The Blind Hunter

Written and illustrated by Kristina Rodanas

Marshall Cavendish
New York

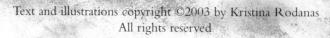

Marshall Cavendish, 99 White Plains Road, Tarrytown, NY 10591
www.marshallcavendish.com

Library of Congress Cataloging-in-Publication Data
Rodanas, Kristina.
The blind hunter / written and illustrated by Kristina Rodanas.
p. cm.
Summary: A blind African hunter teaches a young man how to see by using his other senses.
ISBN 0-7614-5132-3
[1. Blind—Fiction. 2. Senses and sensation—Fiction. 3.
Africa—Fiction. 4. Hunters—Fiction.] I. Title.
PZ7.R5985 Bl 2003
[E]—dc21
2002009049

The text of this book is set in 15-point Bembo.
Book design by Patrice Sheridan
The illustrations were rendered in oil-based colored pencils over watercolor wash.
Printed in China
First edition
6 5 4 3 2 1

For my mother and father who have learned to see with their hearts

Special thanks to Terefe Kerse-McMillin

— Kristina Rodanas

Author's Note

The Blind Hunter was inspired by a story found in Alexander McCall Smith's book of African folktales, *Children of Wax* (Interlink Books).

The story takes place in the southern region of Africa and the characters' names are from the Shona language. Chirobo (chee-ROH-boh) means "the great talker" and Muteye (moo-TAY-ye) is derived from a word meaning "to catch animals in a trap."

I hope the important and timely message of this story will be heard and appreciated by children from many cultures and from many lands.

— Kristina Rodanas

In Africa, not so many years ago, a man named Chirobo lived all by himself in a village of round huts. Each day he went to work in his garden, carefully tending rows of sunflowers, pumpkins, and corn. As he worked he sang sweet songs, and birds of many colors flew out of the trees just to hear him sing.

Chirobo was known to be wise and very kind. People often came to him with questions, for it was said that his answers were never wrong. When children came to visit, he always stopped what he was doing so he could laugh with them and listen to their stories.

Everyone in the village liked this gentle man with the warm smile. Hardly anyone ever seemed to notice that he was blind.

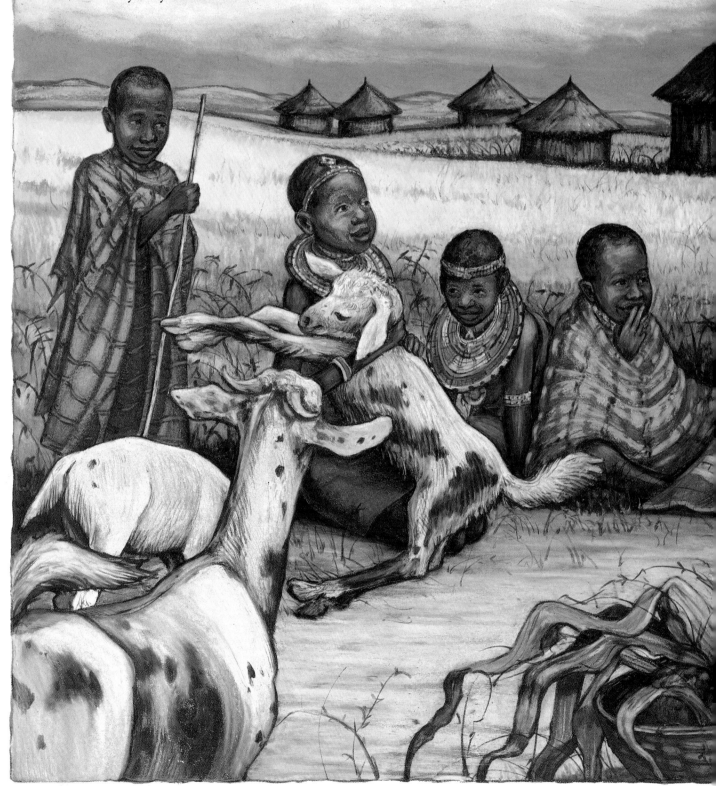

Early one evening, as Chirobo sat stirring a pot of stew, a stranger paused nearby to admire his garden. "Your crops are as beautiful as they are bountiful!" he exclaimed.

Chirobo beamed with pride and asked the young man if he had traveled far. The stranger explained that he was on a hunting trip. He was called Muteye and had come from a village a half day's walk from the west.

"When I return to my home, I will have a sack full of fat birds on my back," he boasted. "Then I will be welcomed as a great hunter!"

"Before my eyes began to fade I, too, was a hunter," said Chirobo. "Come sit with me and eat some of this fine stew. We will have much to talk about."

Muteye gladly accepted Chirobo's offer and joined him beside the cooking fire. He stayed for many hours sharing tales, laughing, and singing.

When the moon had climbed high above the distant trees, the young man got to his feet.

"Thank you, my friend, for your kindness," he said. "Is there anything I can do for you in return?"

Chirobo was silent for a few moments. "It would make me very happy if I could go hunting with you," he replied.

The young man laughed and said, "I will not hunt with a man who cannot see."

"I will be no trouble," Chirobo assured him. "I know how to see in other ways."

"Very well, then," said the young man. "Tomorrow, when the sun rises, we will go hunting. You may use one of my traps. Whatever you catch will be yours to keep."

At the first light of dawn, the two men went out into the bush. The young man led the way, holding the end of a long, straight walking stick. Behind him the blind man followed, clutching the other end. They walked along a narrow path that wound through groves of crooked trees.

All of a sudden, Chirobo pulled back on the walking stick. He
stood stone still, his hands cupped behind his ears. "We must be careful," he whispered. "There is a leopard nearby."

The young man gazed all around but could not see the leopard.
Then he glanced upward, where a strange pattern caught his eye.

Above the path, draped along an acacia limb, a large cat lay sleeping.
When they had safely passed the sleeping beast, Muteye
asked, "How does a man who lives in darkness know when a leopard
is near?"

Chirobo answered simply, "I know how to see with my ears."

The two men walked on without speaking, into a dense forest where the cool air echoed with the sound of a rushing stream. Again Chirobo tugged at the walking stick, stopping in his tracks. He tilted his head and breathed deeply.

"We must be careful," he warned. "There are warthogs around."
The young man looked in all directions but could not see them.

He hurried to the crest of a nearby hill and peered down through the brush. To his surprise, a herd of warthogs trotted into view, their sharp tusks flashing in the midday sun.

After the two hunters had safely passed the wild pigs, Muteye asked, "How does a man who lives in darkness know when there are warthogs about?"

The blind man smiled and said, "I know how to see with my nose."

They continued on into a wide valley that was thick with thorn bushes and the sweet scent of flowers. Once again, Chirobo gave the walking stick a tug and paused, his feet spread wide beneath him. He fell to his knees and placed his hands upon the ground.

"We must be careful," he murmured. "There are rhinos coming this way."

Muteye glanced about the thicket but could not see the rhinos.

Cautiously, he pushed aside the dense bushes and scanned the sur-
rounding landscape. All of a sudden, a pair of rhinos appeared, stomping
through the tall grass.

When the hunters had safely passed the two creatures, the young
man turned and faced his friend. He asked, "How does a man who lives
in darkness know when there are rhinos approaching?"

Quietly, Chirobo gave his answer, "I know how to see with my skin."

Together the men made their way deeper into the valley until they reached a shallow pond. Countless tracks of birds crisscrossed the soft, muddy bank.

"Birds come here for water," observed Muteye. "It is a good place to set our traps."

Following his friend's instructions, Chirobo placed his trap near the edge of the pond while the other man set his trap a short distance away. After he had disguised both traps, the young man said, "We will camp nearby and return tomorrow. Then we will see what we have caught."

That night they talked about many things. Muteye grew to admire the blind man's wisdom and asked him questions about which he had wondered for a long time.

Early the next morning, they returned to their hunting place. Chirobo knew right away that they had been successful. Excited, he cried, "There are birds in our traps. I can hear them!"

The young man checked his own trap first and discovered that he had caught a small, thin quail. Although he was disappointed, he carefully removed it and put it into a goatskin sack. Then he went to check the other trap.

As he kneeled down to look inside, his heart filled with jealousy. The blind man's trap contained a large duck, fat enough to feed a hungry jackal.

For a few moments Muteye hesitated as he considered the two birds and wondered, "How would a man who lives in darkness ever know which bird belonged to him?"

His mind made up, he quickly switched the thin bird for the plump one.

"Your bird is the larger of the two," he said as he handed the quail over to his companion. "It will make a fine meal."

Chirobo stroked the bird's scraggly wings and thoughtfully passed his fingers along its bony back and breast. Without speaking, he put it into his own sack.

Then the men gathered their traps and began the journey back to the village.

In silence they walked and walked, until they stopped to rest beneath an old baobab tree. Muteye was eager to continue the conversation of the night before, so he took the opportunity to ask his friend a question that had worried him since he was a small boy.

"Why do people fight each other?" he inquired.

Chirobo thought about his answer for a long time. When at last he began to speak, his voice was full of sadness.

He said slowly, "People fight because they take from each other what does not belong to them—as you have just done to me."

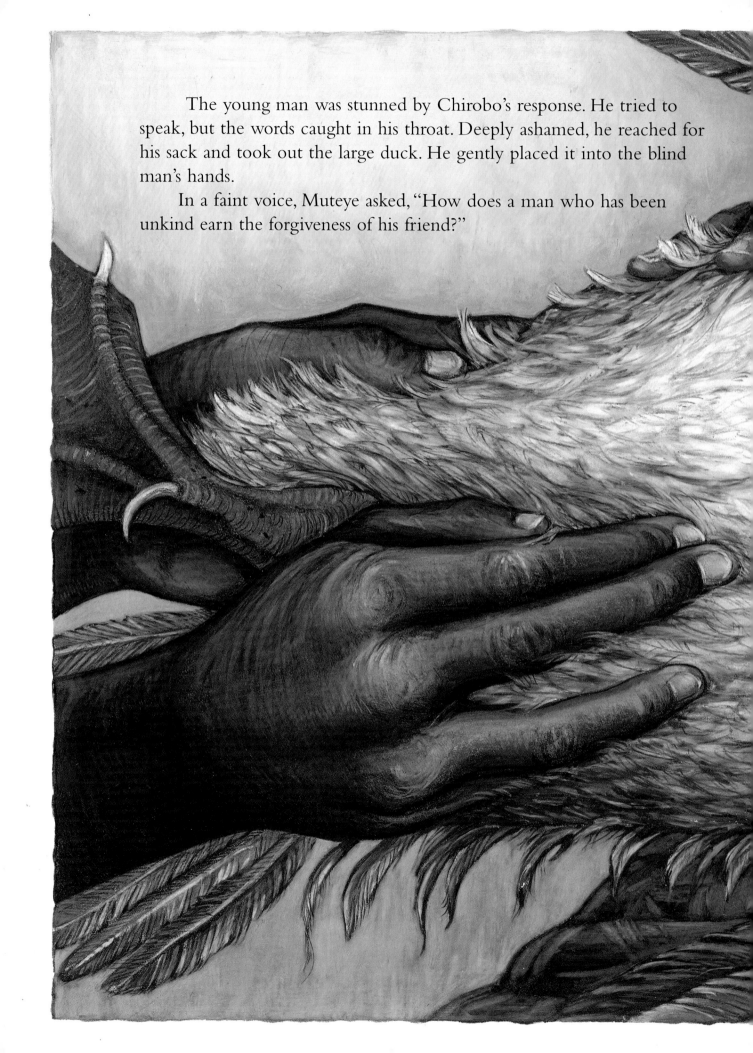

The young man was stunned by Chirobo's response. He tried to speak, but the words caught in his throat. Deeply ashamed, he reached for his sack and took out the large duck. He gently placed it into the blind man's hands.

In a faint voice, Muteye asked, "How does a man who has been unkind earn the forgiveness of his friend?"

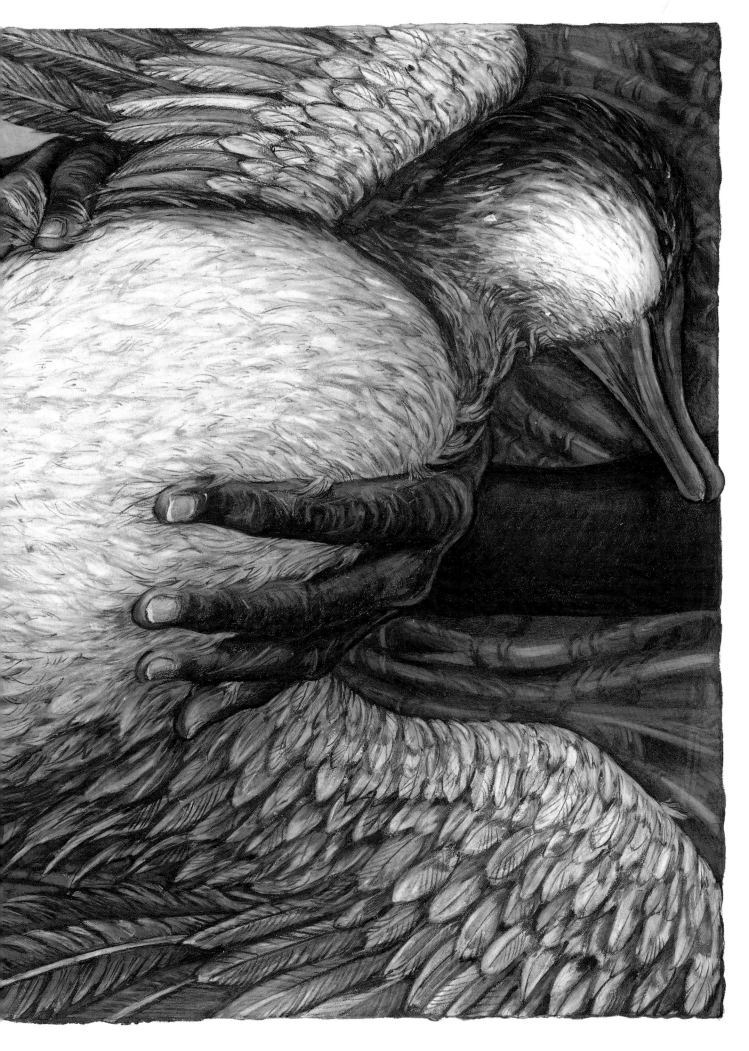

Chirobo's blind eyes seemed to look deep into the young hunter's soul. He said, "By learning to see with his heart—as you have just done with me."